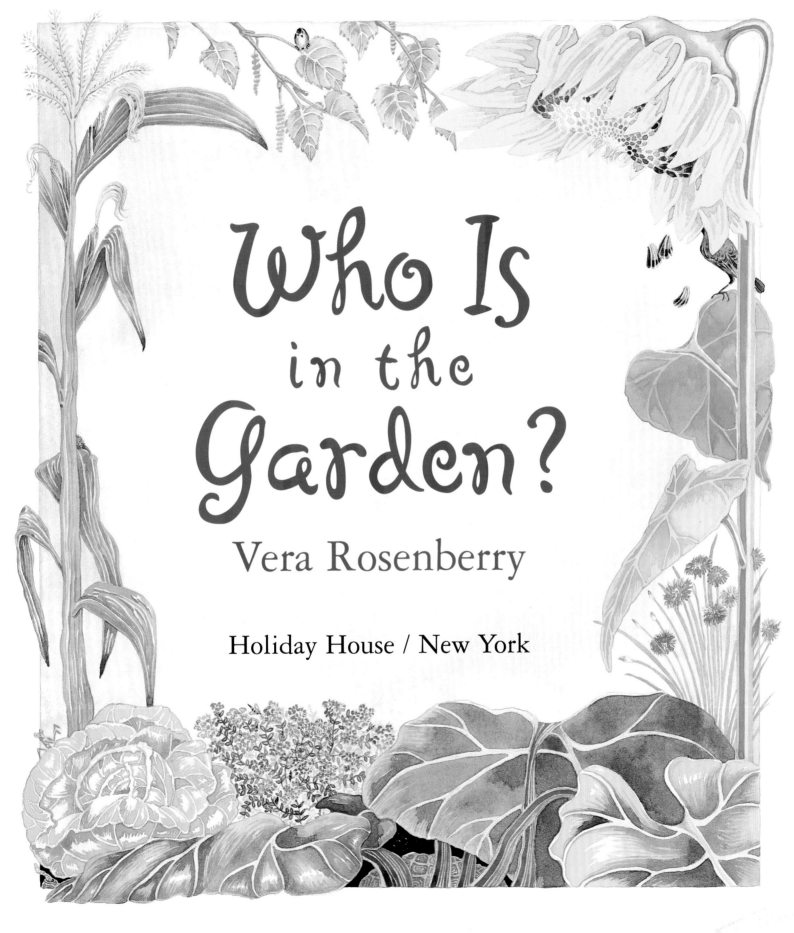

Who Is in the Garden?

Vera Rosenberry

Holiday House / New York

Come into the garden,
through this old gate.

Who is in the garden?

In a tall, slender birch tree
with fluttery leaves
wrens weave their way,
in and out, in and out.

On round, crisp cabbage,
a stiff mantis sits
so still...so still...she hopes
you can't see her.

But you can.

See?
Up in the arbor,
among all the grapes?

That green garter snake
looks just like a vine.

Crowded on bright bushy
butterfly weed,

monarchs sip nectar
through built-in straws.

On a silk-tassled
ear sticking out
of that stalk,

a dainty, brown
field mouse sits,
nibbling corn.

Look under umbrellas
the rhubarb leaves make.
A box turtle
sleeps deep
in the cool shade.

Listen for songs
in the cosmos and thyme
as honeybees hum
to and fro
from their
hives.

EXTENSION

Dig with
this shovel

and you
will find

wiggly pink worms
squiggling all through
the dirt.

Up in the sunflowers,
pecking away,
chattering birds
crack the crunchy,
striped seeds.

Wasps
build a nest
with tiny
wet mudpies.

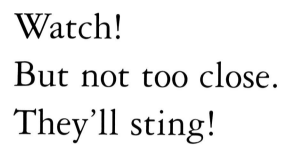

Watch!
But not too close.
They'll sting!

In the trumpet vine flowers,
a red-and-green
FLASH!

A hummingbird darts
and whizzes away.

Crawl into this
twisty-vined,
secret tent.
Long green
beans are
hanging,
and
no one
can see—

who is in the garden.

For Oluka

Copyright © 2001 by Vera Rosenberry

All Rights Reserved

Printed in the United States of America

www.holidayhouse.com

The text typeface is Garamond 3.

The artwork was created with watercolors.

First Edition

Library of Congress Cataloging-in-Publication Data

Rosenberry, Vera.

Who is in the garden? / Vera Rosenberry.

p. cm.

Summary: A tour through a garden

brings encounters with its inhabitants, including wrens,

a praying mantis, a box turtle, and more.

ISBN 0-8234-1529-5

1. Garden animals Juvenile literature.

[1. Garden animals.]

I. Title.

QL119.R68 2001

590—dc21   99-37166

CIP